CONTENTS

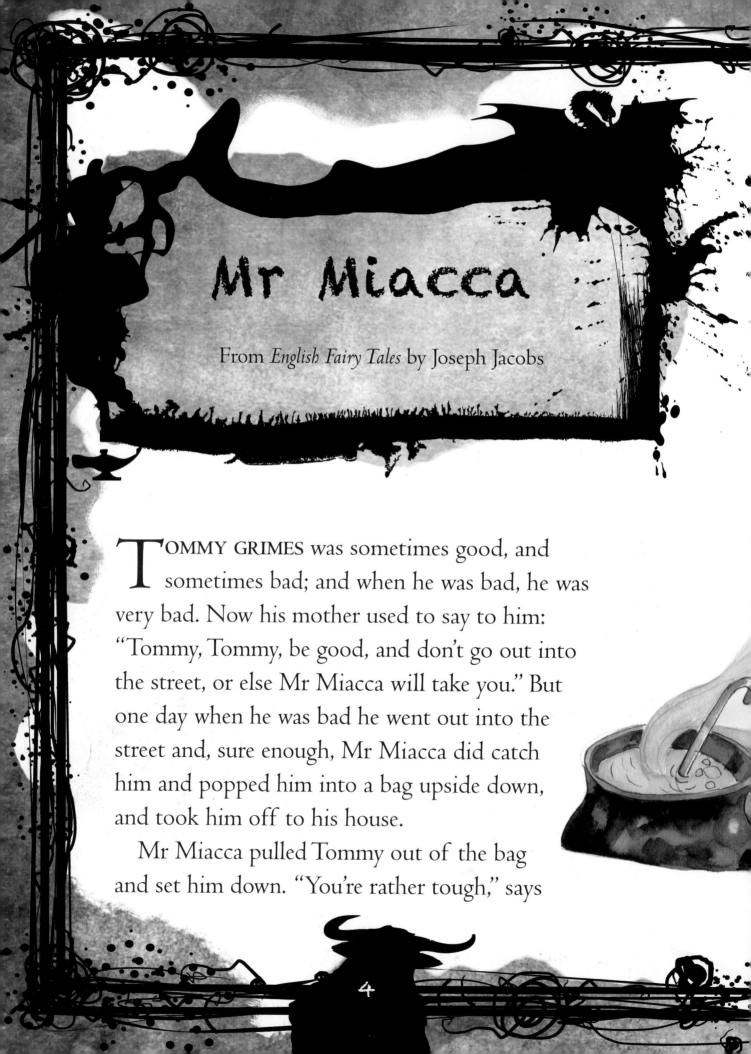

Mr Miacca

From *English Fairy Tales* by Joseph Jacobs

TOMMY GRIMES was sometimes good, and sometimes bad; and when he was bad, he was very bad. Now his mother used to say to him: "Tommy, Tommy, be good, and don't go out into the street, or else Mr Miacca will take you." But one day when he was bad he went out into the street and, sure enough, Mr Miacca did catch him and popped him into a bag upside down, and took him off to his house.

Mr Miacca pulled Tommy out of the bag and set him down. "You're rather tough," says

Scary Fairy Tales

The Prince and the Dragon

and other stories

Compiled by Vic Parker

Miles
KeLLy

First published in 2012 by Miles Kelly Publishing Ltd
Harding's Barn, Bardfield End Green, Thaxted, Essex, CM6 3PX, UK

2 4 6 8 10 9 7 5 3 1

Publishing Director Belinda Gallagher
Creative Director Jo Cowan
Editor Sarah Parkin
Designer Jo Cowan
Editorial Assistants Lauren White, Amy Johnson
Production Manager Elizabeth Collins
Reprographics Stephan Davis, Jennifer Hunt, Thom Allaway

ISBN 978-1-84810-590-4

Printed in China

British Library Cataloguing-in-Publication Data
A catalogue record for this book is available from the British Library

ACKNOWLEDGEMENTS

The publishers would like to thank the following artists who have contributed to this book:

Cover: Cherie Zamazing at The Bright Agency
Advocate Art: Luke Finlayson
The Bright Agency: Si Clark, Peter Cottrill, Gerald Kelley
All other artwork from the Miles Kelly Artwork Bank

The publishers would like to thank the following source for the use of their photographs:
Shutterstock.com (cover) donatas1205, Eky Studio; (page decorations) alarik, dmiskv,
Ensuper, Eugene Ivanov

Every effort has been made to acknowledge the source and copyright holder of each picture.
Miles Kelly Publishing apologises for any unintentional errors or omissions.

Made with paper from a sustainable forest

www.mileskelly.net   info@mileskelly.net

www.factsforprojects.com

he, "but you're all I've got for supper, and you'll not taste bad boiled. But body o' me, I've forgot the herbs." And he called Mrs Miacca.

Mrs Miacca came out of another room and said: "What d'ye want, my dear?"

"Oh, here's a little boy for supper," said Mr Miacca, "and I've forgot the herbs. Mind him, will ye, while I go for them."

"All right, my love," says Mrs Miacca, and off her husband goes.

Then Tommy Grimes said to Mrs Miacca: "Does Mr Miacca always have little boys for supper?"

"Mostly, my dear," said Mrs Miacca, "if little boys are bad enough, and get in his way."

"And don't you have anything else but boy-meat? No pudding?" asked Tommy.

"Ah, I loves pudding," says Mrs Miacca. "But it's not often the likes of me gets pudding."

"Why, my mother is making a pudding this very day," said Tommy Grimes, "shall I run and get some?"

"Now, that's a thoughtful boy," said Mrs Miacca, "only don't be long and be back for supper."

So off Tommy pelters, and right glad he was to get off so cheap; and for many a long day he never went out into the street. But he couldn't always be good; and one day he went out into the street, and as luck would have it, Mr Miacca grabbed him up, popped him in his bag, and took him home.

When Mr Miacca dropped him out; and when he

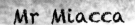

saw him, he said: "Ah, you're the youngster what served me and my missus that shabby trick, leaving us without any supper. Well, you shan't do it again. Here, get under the sofa, and I'll sit on it and wait for the pot to boil for you."

So poor Tommy Grimes had to creep under the sofa, and Mr Miacca sat on it and waited for the pot to boil. And they waited, and they waited, but still the pot didn't boil, till at last Mr Miacca got tired of waiting, and he said: "Here, you under there, I'm not going to wait any longer; put out your leg, and I'll stop your giving us the slip."

So Tommy put out a leg, and Mr Miacca chopped it off, and popped it in the pot.

Suddenly he called for his wife, but nobody answered. So he went into the next room to look for Mrs Miacca, and while he was there, Tommy crept out from under the sofa and ran out of the door, for it was a leg of the sofa that he had put out.

So Tommy Grimes ran home, and never went out into the street until he was old enough to go alone.

The Story of the Fisherman

From *The Arabian Nights Entertainments,*
retold by Andrew Lang

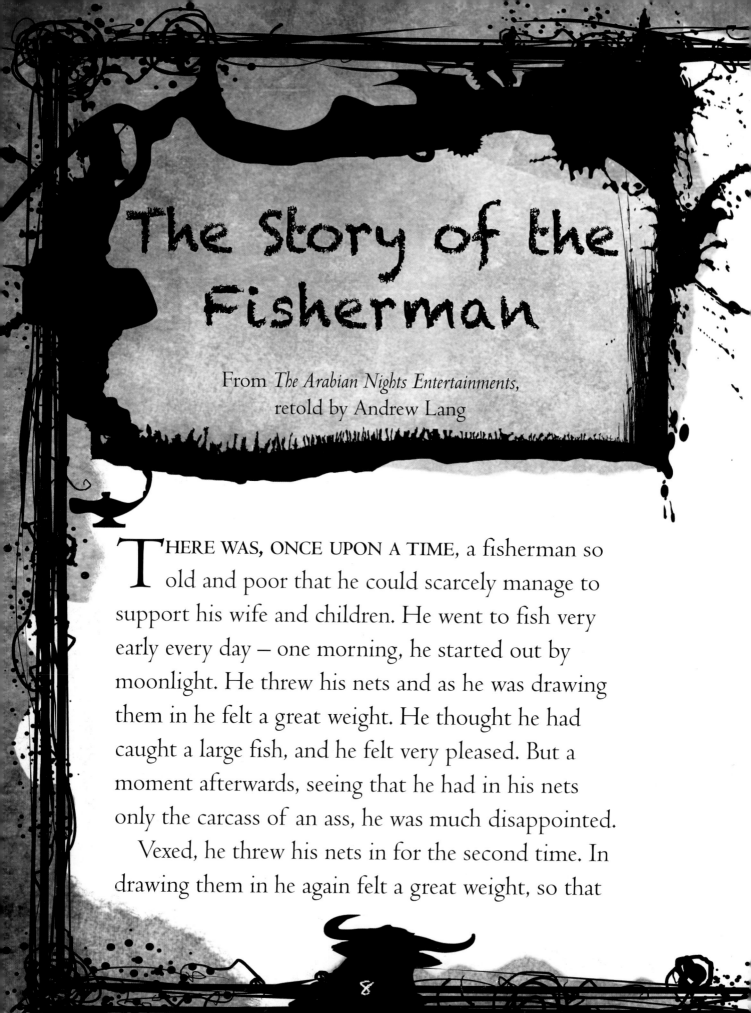

THERE WAS, ONCE UPON A TIME, a fisherman so old and poor that he could scarcely manage to support his wife and children. He went to fish very early every day – one morning, he started out by moonlight. He threw his nets and as he was drawing them in he felt a great weight. He thought he had caught a large fish, and he felt very pleased. But a moment afterwards, seeing that he had in his nets only the carcass of an ass, he was much disappointed.

Vexed, he threw his nets in for the second time. In drawing them in he again felt a great weight, so that he thought they were full of fish. But he found only a large basket full of rubbish. He was much annoyed. "O Fortune," he cried, "do not trifle thus with me!"

So saying, he threw his nets in for the third time. But he only drew in stones, shells and mud. He was almost in despair.

Then he threw his nets for the fourth time. When he thought he had a fish he drew them in with a great deal of trouble. There was no fish, but he found a yellow vase, which by its weight seemed full of something, and he noticed that it was fastened and sealed with lead, with the impression of a seal. The fisherman was delighted. "I will sell it," he said, "and with the money I shall get for it I shall buy a measure of wheat."

He examined the vase on all sides; he shook it to see if it would rattle. But he heard nothing, and so, judging from the impression of the seal and the lid, he thought there must be something precious inside. To find out, he took his knife, and with a little trouble he opened it. He turned it upside down, but nothing came out, which surprised him very much. He set it in front of him, and whilst he was looking at it attentively, such a thick smoke came out that he had to step back a pace or two. This smoke rose up to the clouds and, stretching over the sea and the shore, formed a thick mist. When all the smoke was out of the vase it gathered itself together, and became a thick mass in which appeared a genie, twice as large as the largest giant. When he saw such a terrible-looking monster, the fisherman would liked to have run away, but he trembled so with

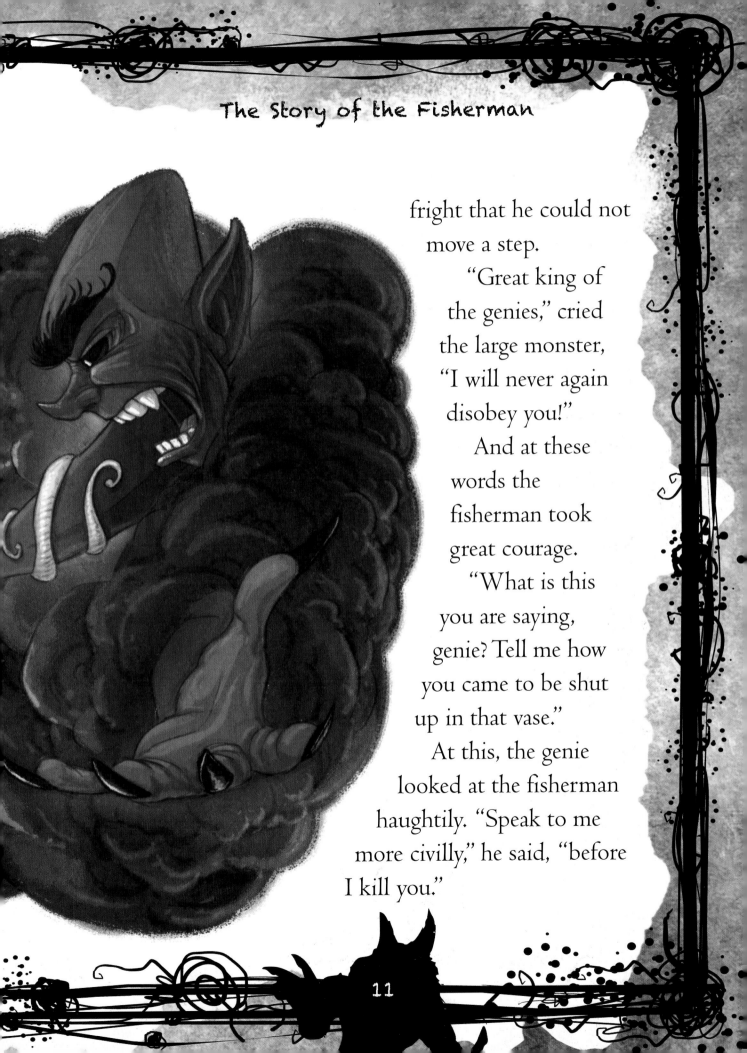

fright that he could not move a step.

"Great king of the genies," cried the large monster, "I will never again disobey you!"

And at these words the fisherman took great courage.

"What is this you are saying, genie? Tell me how you came to be shut up in that vase."

At this, the genie looked at the fisherman haughtily. "Speak to me more civilly," he said, "before I kill you."

"Alas! Why should you kill me?" cried the fisherman. "I have just freed you; have you already forgotten that?"

"No," answered the genie; "but that will not prevent me from killing you; and I am only going to grant you one favour, and that is to choose the manner of your death."

"What have I done to you?" asked the fisherman.

"I cannot treat you in any other way," said the genie, "and if you would know why, listen to my story. I rebelled against the king of the genies. To punish me, he shut me up in this vase of copper, and he put on the leaden seal, which is enchantment enough to prevent my coming out. Then he had the vase thrown into the sea. During the first period of my captivity I vowed that if anyone should free me before a hundred years were passed, I would make him rich even after his death. But that century passed, and no one freed me. In the second century I vowed that I would give all the treasures in the world to my deliverer; but he never came. In the third, I promised

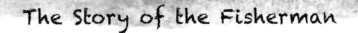

to make him a king, and to grant him three wishes every day; but that century passed away as the other two had done, and I remained in the same plight. At last I grew angry at being captive for so long, and I vowed that if anyone would release me I would kill him at once, and would only allow him to choose in what manner he should die. So you see, as you have freed me today, choose in what way you will die."

The fisherman was very unhappy. "What an unlucky man I am to have freed you! I implore you to spare my life."

"I have told you," said the genie, "that it is impossible. Choose quickly; you are wasting time."

The fisherman began to devise a plot.

"Since I must die," he said, "before I choose the manner of my death, I conjure you on your honour to tell me if you really were in that vase?"

"Yes, I was," answered the genie.

"I really cannot believe it," said the fisherman. "That vase could not contain one of your feet even, and how could your whole body go in? I cannot believe it unless I see you do it."

Then the genie began to change himself into smoke, which, as before, spread over the sea and the shore, and which, then collecting itself together, began to go back into the vase slowly and evenly till there was nothing left outside. Then a voice came from the vase which said to the fisherman, "Well, unbelieving fisherman, here I am in the vase; do you believe me now?"

The fisherman, instead of answering, took the lid of lead and shut it down quickly on the vase.

"Now, O genie," he cried, "ask pardon of me, and choose by what death you will die! But no, it will be better if I throw you into the sea whence I drew you out, and I will build a house on the shore to warn fishermen who come to cast their nets here, against fishing up such a wicked genie as you are, who vows to kill the man who frees you."

At these words the genie did all he could to get out, but he could not, because of the enchantment of the lid.

The Prince and the Dragon

From Andrew Lang's *Crimson Fairy Book*

ONCE UPON A TIME there lived an emperor who had three sons. They were all fine young men, who were very fond of hunting.

One morning the eldest mounted his horse and set out for a forest where wild animals of all sorts were to be found. He had not long left the castle, when a hare sprang out of a thicket and dashed across the road in front. The young man gave chase, till at last the hare took refuge in a mill by the side of a river. The prince entered the mill, but stopped in terror, for before him stood a dragon, breathing flames. At this

fearful sight the prince turned to fly, but a fiery tongue coiled round his waist, and drew him into the dragon's mouth, and he was seen no more.

A week passed, and when the prince never came back everyone in the town began to grow uneasy. At last his next brother told the emperor that he likewise would go out to hunt, and that perhaps he would find some clue as to his brother's disappearance. Hardly had the castle gates closed than the hare sprang out of the bushes as before, and led the huntsman to the mill. There stood a dragon breathing flames; and out shot a fiery tongue which coiled round the prince's waist, and lifted him into the dragon's mouth, and he was seen no more.

Days went by, and the emperor waited for the sons who never came. His youngest son wished to go in search of his brothers, but for a long time the emperor refused to listen, lest he should lose him also. But the prince begged so hard, that at length the emperor agreed.

The young prince started on his way, and no

sooner was he outside the city than a hare sprang out of the bushes. But this time he was not followed by the prince. Wiser than his brothers, the young man turned away, saying: "There are as good hares in the forest, and when I have caught them, I can come back and look for you."

For many hours he rode up and down the mountain, but saw nothing, and at last he came to the mill. Here he found an old woman sitting, whom he greeted pleasantly.

"Good morning to you, little mother," he said.

And the old woman answered: "Good morning, my son.'"

"Tell me, little mother," went on the prince, "where shall I find my hare?"

"My son," replied the old woman, "that was no hare, but a dragon who has led many men hither, and then has eaten them all."

At these words the prince's heart grew heavy, and he cried, "Then my brothers must have come here, and have been eaten!"

"You have guessed right," answered the old woman; "and you should go home at once, before the same fate overtakes you."

"Will you not come with me out of this dreadful place?" said the young man.

"He took me prisoner, too," answered she, "and I cannot shake off his chains."

"Then listen to me," cried the prince. "When the dragon comes back, ask him where he always goes when he leaves here, and what makes him so strong."

So the prince went home, and the old woman remained at the mill, and as soon as the dragon returned she said to him: "Where have you been all this time?"

"I have travelled far," answered he.

Then the old woman said: "I have wondered so often where you get your strength from; I do wish you would tell me."

The dragon answered: "My strength lies far away; so far that you could never reach it. Far, far from here is a kingdom, and by its capital city is a lake, and in

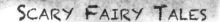
the lake is a dragon, and inside the dragon
is a wild boar, and inside the wild boar
a hare, and inside the hare a pigeon,
and inside the pigeon a sparrow, and
inside the sparrow is my strength."

The following morning, when
the dragon had left the mill,
the prince came back, and
the old woman told him
everything that the
creature had said. He
listened in silence,
and then returned to
the castle, where he
put on a suit of
shepherd's clothes,
and he went forth
to seek a place as
tender of sheep.

For some time
he wandered, till he

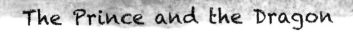

came to a large city in a distant kingdom, surrounded on three sides by a great lake, which happened to be the very lake in which the dragon lived. The prince presented himself at the palace, and when he knelt before the emperor, His Majesty said: "Outside the city walls you will find a large lake, and by its banks lie the richest meadows in my kingdom. When you are leading out your flocks to pasture, they will run straight to these meadows, and none that have gone there have ever come back. Take heed, therefore, my son."

With a low bow the prince promised to do his best. Then he went to the market place, where he bought two greyhounds, a hawk and a set of pipes; after that he took the sheep out to pasture. The instant the animals caught sight of the lake, they trotted off as fast as their legs would go to the green meadows round it. The prince did not try to stop them; he only placed his hawk on the branch of a tree, laid his pipes on the grass, and bade the greyhounds sit still; then, rolling up his sleeves and trousers, he waded into the water crying as he did so: "Dragon! If you are not a coward, come out and fight with me!"

"I am waiting for you, O prince;" and the dragon reared out of the water, huge and horrible to see.

The prince sprang upon him and they grappled with each other and fought together till the sun was high, and it was noon. Then the dragon gasped: "O prince, let me dip my burning head once into the lake, and I will hurl you up to the sky."

But the prince answered, "Oh ho, my good dragon, do not crow too soon! If the emperor's daughter were only here, and would kiss me on the forehead, I would throw you up higher still!" And suddenly the dragon's hold loosened and he fell back into the lake.

As soon as it was evening, the prince washed away all signs of the fight, took his hawk upon his shoulder, and his pipes under his arm, and with his greyhounds in front and his flock following after him, he set out for the city. As they passed through the streets the people stared in wonder, for never

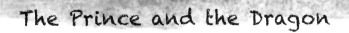

before had any flock returned from the lake.

The next morning he rose early and led his sheep down to the lake. This time, however, the emperor sent two men on horseback, with orders to watch without being seen. As soon as the shepherd reached the place he laid, as before, his pipes on the grass and bade the greyhounds sit beside them, while the hawk he perched on the branch of the tree. Then he rolled up his trousers and his sleeves, and waded into the water crying: "Dragon! If you are not a coward, come out and fight with me!"

And the dragon answered: "I am waiting for you, O prince," and he reared out of the water, huge and horrible to see. Again they clasped each other tight and fought till it was noon, and when the sun was at its hottest, the dragon gasped: "O prince, let me dip my burning head once in the lake, and I will hurl you up to the sky."

But the prince answered: "Oh ho, my good dragon, do not crow too soon! If the emperor's daughter were only here, and would kiss me on the forehead, I would throw you up higher still!" And suddenly the dragon's hold loosened and he fell back into the lake.

As soon as it was evening the prince again collected his sheep and, playing on his pipes, he marched before them into the city.

Meanwhile the two horsemen had ridden quickly back and told the emperor all. The emperor then called his daughter to him and repeated it to her. "Tomorrow," he said, when he had finished, "you shall go with the shepherd to the lake, and you shall kiss him on the forehead as he wishes."

Scarcely had the sun begun to peep over the hills next morning, when the princess stood by the shepherd's side, ready to go to the lake.

Merrily the shepherd blew on his pipes as he marched at the head of his flock.

And so they reached the lake.

In an instant the sheep were scattered, and the prince placed his hawk on the tree, and his pipes on the grass, while he bade his greyhounds lie beside them. Then he rolled up his trousers and his sleeves,

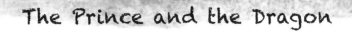

and waded into the water, calling: "Dragon! If you are not a coward, come forth, and let us have one more fight together."

And the dragon answered: "I am waiting for you, O prince," and reared out of the water, huge and horrible to see. Swiftly he drew near to the bank, and the prince sprang to meet him, and they grasped each other and fought till it was noon. And when the sun was at its hottest, the dragon cried: "O prince, let me dip my burning head in the lake, and I will hurl you to the sky."

But the prince answered: "Oh ho, my good dragon, do not crow too soon! If the emperor's daughter were only here, and she would kiss my forehead, I would throw you higher still."

Hardly had he spoken, when the princess, who had been listening, ran up and kissed him on the forehead. Then the prince swung the dragon straight up into the clouds, and when he touched the earth again, he broke into a thousand pieces. Out of the pieces there sprang a wild boar and it galloped away,

but the prince called his hounds to give chase, and they caught the boar and tore it to bits. Out of the pieces there sprang a hare, and in a moment the greyhounds were after it, and they caught it and killed it; and out of the hare there came a pigeon. Quickly the prince let loose his hawk, which

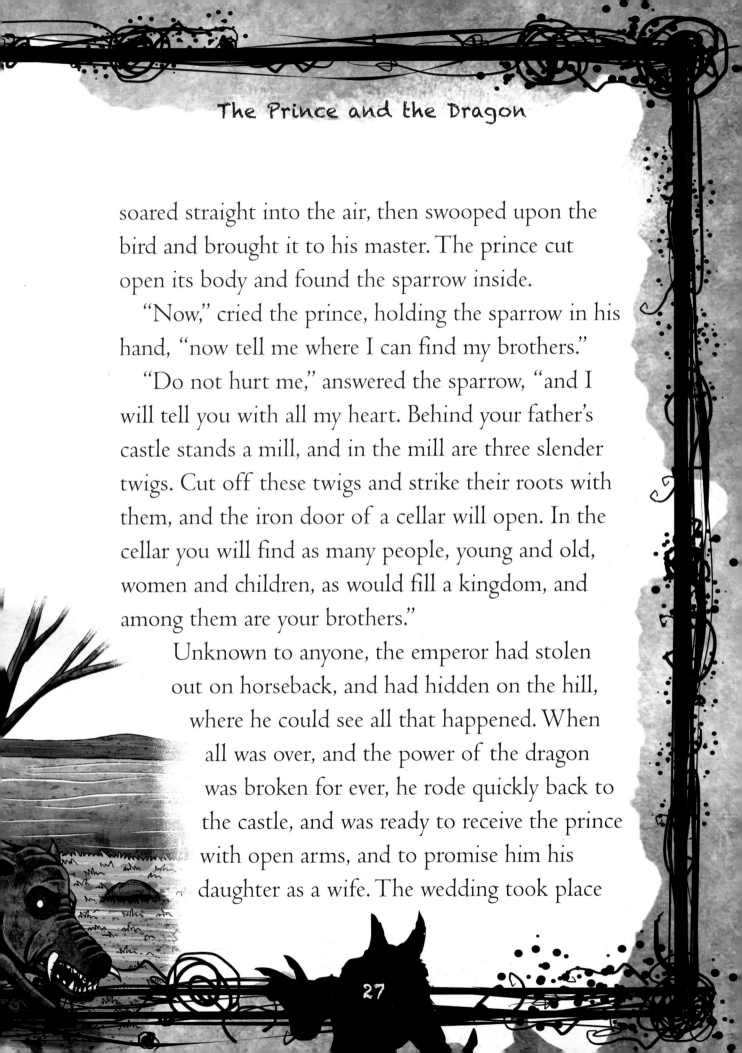

soared straight into the air, then swooped upon the bird and brought it to his master. The prince cut open its body and found the sparrow inside.

"Now," cried the prince, holding the sparrow in his hand, "now tell me where I can find my brothers."

"Do not hurt me," answered the sparrow, "and I will tell you with all my heart. Behind your father's castle stands a mill, and in the mill are three slender twigs. Cut off these twigs and strike their roots with them, and the iron door of a cellar will open. In the cellar you will find as many people, young and old, women and children, as would fill a kingdom, and among them are your brothers."

Unknown to anyone, the emperor had stolen out on horseback, and had hidden on the hill, where he could see all that happened. When all was over, and the power of the dragon was broken for ever, he rode quickly back to the castle, and was ready to receive the prince with open arms, and to promise him his daughter as a wife. The wedding took place with great splendour, and for a whole week the town was hung with coloured lamps, and tables were spread in the hall of the castle for all who chose to come and eat. And when the feast was over, the prince told the emperor and the people who he really was, and everyone rejoiced still more, and preparations were made for the prince and princess to return to their own kingdom, for the prince was impatient to set free his brothers.

The first thing he did when he reached his native country was to hasten to the mill, where he found the three twigs as the sparrow had told him. The moment that he struck their roots the iron door flew open, and from the cellar a countless multitude of men and women streamed forth. He bade them go one by one wheresoever they would, while he waited by the door till his brothers passed through. How delighted they were to meet again, and to hear all that the prince had done to deliver them. And they went home and served him all the days of their lives, for they said that only he was fit to be king.

Molly Whuppie

From *English Fairy Tales* by Joseph Jacobs

ONCE UPON A TIME there was a man and a wife who had too many children, and they could not get food for them, so they took the three youngest and left them in a deep, dark wood. The girls travelled and travelled and could see never a house. Evening drew in and they were hungry. At last they saw a light and made for it; it turned out to be a big, old house. They knocked at the door and a woman came to it who said: "What do you want?"

"Please let us in and give us something to eat," the three desperate girls implored.

The woman said: "I can't do that, as my man is a giant, and he would kill you if he comes home."

"Let us stop for just a little while," they begged, "and we will go away before he comes."

Then the woman took pity on them, and took them in, and set them down before the fire, and gave them milk and bread.

But just as they had begun to eat, a great knock came to the door, and a dreadful voice said: "Fee, fie, fo, fum, I smell the blood of some earthly one. Who have you there, wife?"

"Eh," said the wife, "it's three poor lassies cold and hungry, and they will go away. Ye won't touch 'em."

The giant said nothing, but ate up a big supper, and ordered them to stay all night.

Now the giant had three lassies of his own, and the three travellers were to sleep in the same bed with them. The youngest of the guests was called Molly Whuppie, and she was very clever. She noticed that before they went to bed the giant put straw ropes round her neck and her sisters', but that round his

own lassies' necks he put gold chains. So Molly took care and did not fall asleep, but waited till she was sure everyone was sleeping sound. Then she slipped out of the bed, and took the straw ropes off her own and her sisters' necks, and took the gold chains off the giant's lassies. She then put the straw ropes on the giant's lassies and the gold chains on herself and her sisters, and lay down.

And in the middle of the night up rose the giant, armed with a great club, and he felt for the necks with the straw. It was dark as pitch. He took his own lassies out of bed on to the floor, and battered them until they were dead, and then lay down again, thinking he had managed fine.

Molly thought it time she and her sisters were out of that, so she wakened them and told them to be quiet, and they slipped out of the house. They all got out safe, and they ran and ran, and never stopped until morning, when they saw a grand house before them. It turned out to be a king's house: so Molly went in, and told her story to the king. He said: "Well, Molly, you are a clever girl, and you have managed well; but, if you would manage better, and go back, and steal the giant's sword that hangs on the back of his bed, then I will give your eldest sister my eldest son to marry." Molly said she would try.

So she went back, and managed to slip into the giant's house, and crept in below the bed. The giant came home, and ate up a great supper, and went to bed. Molly waited until he was snoring, and she crept out, and reached over the giant and got down the sword; but just as she got it out over the bed it gave a rattle, and up jumped the giant, and Molly ran out the door, the sword with her; and she ran, and he ran, till they came to a long, rickety, old bridge called the Bridge of One Hair; and she got over, but the hefty giant couldn't.

So Molly took the sword to the king, and her sister was married to his son. And the king, he says: "Ye've managed well, Molly; but if ye would manage better, and steal the purse that lies below the giant's pillow, I would marry your second sister to my second son." And Molly said she would try.

So she set out for the giant's house, and slipped in, and hid again below the bed, and waited till the giant had eaten his supper, and was snoring sound asleep. She slipped out, and slipped her hand below the pillow, and got out the purse; but just as she was going out the giant wakened, and ran after her; and she ran, and he ran, till they came to the Bridge of One Hair and she got over, but he couldn't.

So Molly took the purse to the king, and her

second sister was married to the king's second son. After that the king says to Molly: "Molly, you are a clever girl, but if you would do better yet, and steal the giant's ring that he wears on his finger, I will give you my youngest son for yourself." Molly said she would try.

So back she goes to the house, and hides herself below the bed. The giant wasn't long ere he came home, and, after he had eaten a great big supper, he went to his bed, and shortly was snoring loud. Molly crept out and reached over the bed, and got hold of the giant's hand, and she pulled and she pulled until she got off the ring; but just as she got it off the giant got up, and gripped her by the hand, and he says: "Now I have caught you, Molly

Whuppie, and, if I had done as much ill to you as ye have done to me, what would ye do to me?"

Molly says: "I would put you into a sack, and I'd put the cat and the dog beside you, and a needle and thread and shears, and I'd hang you up upon the wall, and I'd go to the wood, and choose the thickest stick I could get, and I would come home, and take you down, and bang you till you were dead."

"Well, Molly," says the giant, "I'll do that to you."

So he gets a sack, and puts Molly into it, and the cat and the dog beside her, and a needle and thread and shears, and hangs her up upon the wall, and goes to the wood to choose a stick.

Molly, she sings out: "Oh, if ye saw what I see."

"Oh," says the giant's wife, "what do ye see?"

But Molly never said a word but, "Oh, if ye saw what I see!"

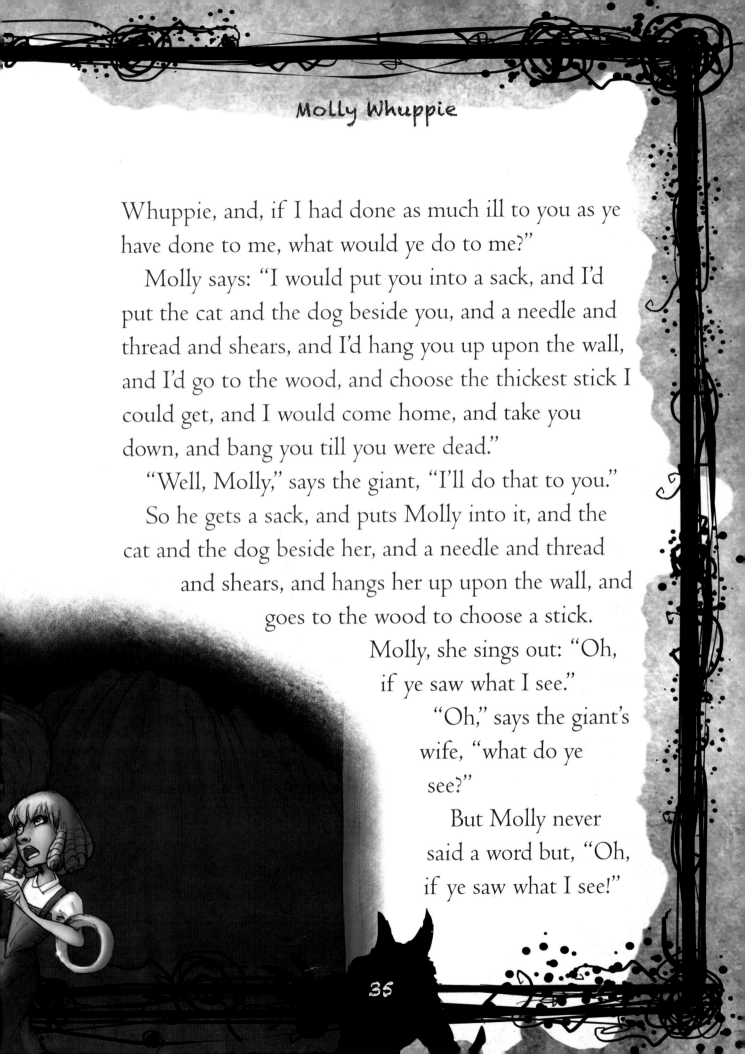

The giant's wife begged that Molly would take her up into the sack till she would see what Molly saw. So Molly took the shears and cut a hole in the sack, and took out the needle and thread with her and jumped down, and helped the giant's wife up into the sack, and sewed up the hole.

The giant's wife saw nothing, and began to ask to get down again; but Molly took no notice and hid herself behind the door.

Home came the giant, with a great big tree in his hand, and he took down the sack, and began to batter it. His wife cried, "It's me, man;" but the dog barked and the cat mewed, and he did not know his wife's voice. But Molly came out from behind the door, and the giant saw her, and he ran after her; and she ran and he ran, till they came to the Bridge of One Hair, and she got over but he couldn't.

So Molly took the ring to the king, and she was married to his youngest son, and she never saw the giant again.

The Singing Bone

By the Brothers Grimm

IN A CERTAIN COUNTRY there was once great lamentation over a wild boar that laid waste the farmer's fields and killed the cattle. The beast was so big and strong that no one dared to go near the forest in which it lived. At last the king gave notice that whosoever should capture or kill the wild boar should have his only daughter for his wife.

Now there lived in the country two brothers who declared themselves willing to undertake the hazardous enterprise; the elder was crafty and shrewd; the younger was innocent and simple.

The king said, "In order that you may be the more sure of finding the beast, you must go into the forest from opposite sides."

When the younger had gone a short way, a little man stepped up to him. He held in his hand a spear and said, "I give you this spear because your heart is pure and good; with this you can boldly attack the wild boar, and it will do you no harm."

The younger brother thanked the little man, shouldered the spear, and went on fearlessly.

Before long he saw the beast, which rushed at him; but he held the spear towards it, and it ran so swiftly against it that its heart was split in two. Then he took the monster on his back and went homewards with it to the king.

As he came out at the other side of the forest, there stood at the entrance a house where people were making merry with wine and dancing. His elder brother had gone in here to drink until he felt brave.

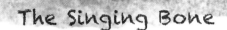

But when he saw his young brother coming out of the forest laden with his booty, his envious, evil heart gave him no peace. He called out to him, "Come in, dear brother, rest and refresh yourself."

The youth, who suspected no evil, went in and told him about the man who had given him the spear.

The elder brother kept him there until the evening, and then they went away together, and when in the darkness they came to a bridge over a brook, the elder brother let the other go first. When the younger brother was halfway across, the elder brother gave him such a blow from behind that the younger fell down dead.

The elder buried him beneath the bridge, took the boar, and carried it to the king, pretending that he had killed it. And when his younger brother did not come back he said, "The boar must have killed

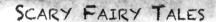

him," and every one believed it.

Years afterwards a shepherd was driving his herd across the bridge, and saw lying in the sand beneath, a little bone. He thought that it would make a good mouthpiece, so he clambered down, picked it up, and cut out of it a mouthpiece for his horn. But when he blew through it, the bone began to sing:

"Ah, friend, thou blowest upon my bone!
Long have I lain beside the water;
My brother slew me for the boar,
And took for his wife the king's daughter."

"What a wonderful horn!" said the shepherd. "I must take it to my lord the king." And when he came with it to the king the horn again began to sing its little song. The king understood it all, and caused the ground below the bridge to be dug up, and then the whole skeleton of the murdered man came to light. The wicked brother could not deny the deed, and was sewn up in a sack and drowned. But the bones of the murdered man were laid to rest in a beautiful tomb in the churchyard.